THE HIDDEN FOREST

THE HIDDEN FOREST

TEXT
BY
SIGURD F. OLSON

PHOTOGRAPHS
BY
LES BLACKLOCK

A STUDIO BOOK
THE VIKING PRESS • NEW YORK

ACKNOWLEDGMENTS

The authors wish to express their appreciation to Nicolas Ducrot, whose contagious enthusiasm, deep awareness, and artistic perception spurred us on; to Ann Langen for editing and preparing the essays; and to Elizabeth Olson and Frances Blacklock for their constant encouragement, understanding, and faith.

First published in 1969 by The Viking Press, Inc.
625 Madison Avenue, New York, N.Y. 10022

Published simultaneously in Canada by
The Macmillan Company of Canada Limited

Library of Congress catalog card number: 70-83796

Printed and bound in Switzerland
by C.J. Bucher Ltd., Lucerne

CONTENTS

To Elizabeth and Frances

INTRODUCTION

Engrossed with the grand sweep of scenic vistas, valleys, rivers, lakes, and bogs, most people see the woods as a hawk soaring far above might see them. This broad over-all view is possibly the best way to approach the enjoyment of any terrain. Such a view, however, is only part of the picture, for this vastness hides a multitude of little things close to the earth, fungi and lichens, mosses and flowers, skeins of spider webs, dewdrops on grasses and leaves, the waxy shine of opening buds, a veritable host of hidden beauties on the forest floor.

The forest depends on an unseen world of viruses, molds, and bacteria, and the smaller forms of life they nurture. All begins and ends here beneath the trees, and those who are not aware, who have only the grand point of view, miss the intimate matrix of the design itself.

A granite cliff has beauty all its own, a bold dramatic symbol of evolving earth structure. Within it is a universe of living crystals, and outside, a growing community of forms which have found a a place to live on its roughened surfaces. One who sees it as only a cliff knows little of the part it plays in the great plan.

Only by looking closely can we begin to understand and appreciate the intimate interrelationship of all living things to one another and to the earth. It is impossible in a book so brief to more than hint at the complexity of the pattern. We can, however, through pictures chosen not only for their beauty but also for their meaning, open the door to a vision of the forest world of which all life is an inseparable part.

A glimpse of snow dripping off the end of a spruce branch in late winter reveals the entire drama of cyclic change, of weather wisdom and meteorology, of the powerful surge of awakening life and growth.

A flower in the spring tells the story of all flowers, and within its color and perfection lies the phenomenon of evolution and adaptation to environment.

A mushroom sprouting after a summer's rain speaks of the multiplicity of forms waiting only for the proper warmth and moisture to encourage them to emerge and scatter spores or seeds.

A reddened leaf in the fall is more than a gorgeous color against the sky; it is the story of fulfillment, death, and decay.

A wing mark or a track on the winter's snow is evidence that though the cold has come, life goes on and, through waiting, fulfills a purpose just as it does in the seasons of growth.

This book is no scientific tome, cross-indexed, documented, and replete with awesome Latin names. It is simply a guide to a world available to all, a vision possible to anyone with an open and receptive mind. It is far more important to know the lift of spirit when one sees the first sky-blue flowers of hepatica, or mayflower, than to be overly concerned with terminology. To grasp through the simple medium of discovery and delight the broad meanings of the almost unknown design on the forest floor is better than to lose appreciation through lack of awareness and understanding.

PAGES 9-12

9. Old fire scars at the bases of towering red pines are a key to the mysteries of growth, survival, and death in the forest.

10-11. Rocky lakeshores and islands, gnarled pines and spruces, lichen-covered ledges, and beds of humus and duff shelter myriads of living things.

12. In a bold splash of yellow and green beside the flooded creek, marsh marigolds speak of the lushness and surging life of spring.

SPRING

THE MIRACLE OF SPRING

One has to live in the north all winter to appreciate the coming of spring. Without knowing the long white months, the deep snows and storms with their bitter cold, the longing, hoping, and waiting for the first warm zephyrs from the south, one cannot begin to understand the miracle—for a miracle it is, the grandest and most exciting in nature.

Toward the end of March, when warm breezes begin to blow, I stand unbelievingly, breathing them in, senses open, my entire being hungry and perceptive, pores absorbing every nuance, nerve ends reveling in every hint of change. Words cannot explain or describe the experience of standing in simple adoration, marveling at the aliveness of a drop of water hanging from the end of a spruce tip, at the first sight of living brown earth and open water in a creek. Birches are touched swiftly with the first of the warming colors, and horizons are softened by subtle shades different from the stark whiteness of winter.

A few weeks later, when the snow is nearly gone and the sun has had its way, we must climb the highest hill and see the sweep of the land to get the full impact of what is happening. Now there are broad brushstrokes of Nile green with washes of silver gray over the aspen-covered hills and a rosiness where maples are bursting into flower. From thousands of square miles of balsam, spruce, and pine, new smells fill the air: waves of clean resin, the rich odor of thawing earth and of the mold of damp leaves.

Come down now into the valleys, find a little creek tumbling over the rocks, see its white lacework as it foams over ledges with mosses, lichens, and ferns springing almost full-grown beside it. This is no time to dawdle and wait. Plants must grow fast lest summer and fall catch them without flowers or buds. There will be no second chance.

The creek widens and slows through a beaver pond, and I hear its trickle through the interlaced branches of the dam at its lower end. The placid water is sky-blue, bordered by pussy willows, by clusters of dogwood with blazing red stems, and by alder golden with pollen. Frogs are laying eggs; glutinous masses of them float in the shallows. Birds are establishing nesting sites around the pond. A pair of red-winged blackbirds carols from the cattails, the male flaunting its crimson epaulets for all to see. A tiny pert marsh wren is singing its heart out from a thicket of dwarf birch. Swallows resplendent in their purple iridescence and creamy white soar over the water, catching the first insects. The swamp belongs to them. Life is awakening; movement and change are in the air.

As I peer into a shallow bay of the pool, my face close to the surface, for a moment I see nothing but the reflections of clouds, but as my eyes become accustomed to the water and its brown leaf-strewn bottom, I see many things: a mosquito larva jerking and wriggling to the surface for air, a caddis worm climbing sedately up a stem with its back-borne camouflage of tiny bits of grass and grains of sand, a diving beetle with a tail-held silver bubble, a newly hatched tadpole scurrying over the mud.

That little backwater, with its reflection of sky, its greening grass, horsetails and ferns all but bursting out of the newly warmed muck, and the lush leaves of cowslips, is loveliness itself. It is far more than this, however, for within it is the very spirit of spring, evidence of nature's fecundity and her ability to produce endlessly wherever there are water, food, and returning warmth. Here is the story of resurrection.

As I sit beside the pool, I hear the drumming of a grouse. The sound seems to come from everywhere, a strange drumroll that engulfs all other sounds, starting with a slow, rather muffled beat, working up to a crescendo that fills the air with heady and resonant booming. I remember a different world of a few months ago, and a grouse exploding out of a snowbank, the tips of its wings marking its hiding place. The bird flew to the top of a brittle frozen aspen, and I watched its precarious budding, wondering if it would survive the owls and weasels and the temperatures of thirty and forty degrees below zero.

In that throbbing accolade to spring is proof it has survived. The bird is not far away, and I can picture it strutting up and down a log, spreading its gorgeous fantail in all its russet glory, dragging its stiff wingtips, rearing back as far as it dares before starting the dignified beating that may bring some demure and fluttering female, or possibly an owl or a prowling fox. No other sound in the north catches so effectively the very essence of spring, of flowing water in the creeks, of placid ponds bursting with life, of budding trees and flowers and the softness spreading over the once-frozen land.

Perhaps more important than anything else is the consciousness of flowing water. To one who has seen only ice, water frozen into rigidity, for half a year, the actual awareness of movement and all it implies, compounded with its music as it cascades over rocks or trickles through a beaver dam, is a miracle indeed, and a priceless privilege in today's busy world.

TIME OF FLOWERS

It was a day in late March, and a purplish blush was spreading over the tops of the birches. Though the snow was still deep, something was happening to that hillside, something compounded by a gentleness in the wind and a sun that was higher now, and warm.

Along the edge of a swamp I found a stem of red ozier dogwood, bright and gay against the whiteness of the snow; willows along a frozen creek actually were swelling and responding to some influence deep below. On the south slope of a hill grown with jackpine and spruce, I saw a branch dripping with melting snow, and even as I marveled at the miracle of running water, the sun went under a cloud and the dripping changed to ice.

A few weeks later, when the creek was flush with water from the sinking drifts, though the willows were still all but buried, the first pussy willows were out in silvery splendor. The big shiny buds of Balm-of-Gilead poplar just beyond were also growing large, and I picked one, crushing it in my hand, and caught the scent of resin that soon would make the entire valley fragrant.

Following the creek one day in May, I came upon a swampy flat covered with marsh marigolds, the flowers of spring floods. The butter-yellow blossoms spread far into the woods, covering the forest floor beneath a stand of black ash trees. I picked a cluster and admired the broad waxy leaves and the lush petals. To me these lowly cowslips, as many call them, really speak of spring, bringing back memories of the nameless little creeks of my boyhood. Long ago I learned those clean, crisp leaves not only made a fine bed for the speckles in my creel, but somehow complemented their beauty. To be sure, one could lay trout on grass or moss, but there was always a residue of bits of debris, dead stems, and broken moss ends that marred the delicate mottling of the fish and the jewel-like spots along their sides. Cowslip leaves kept them clean and firm, and after all there was something to be said for tradition.

All this flooded back to me as I saw the expanse of color. That yellow sweep looked as though an artist had caught the wild, free feeling of spring in one breathtaking splash of gold. I like such carefree boldness wherever it is found: broad unfettered stretches, a dappled forest floor sprinkled with the white of trillium against last year's brown leaves of maple and oak, blue harebells against the gray massiveness of a cliff.

In the spring I look at the forest floor with excitement, no matter how dead it may appear to be, for life is there, waiting for the signal to emerge. The trees play their part in protection and control, providing a constant supply of leaves and branches for humus, but they change slowly and respond little from season to season, except in their colors in spring and fall. Not so with the smaller flowering plants, for their time is short. The floor is a veritable storehouse of living things, a promise for the future, a security against the disasters of fire, wind, and storm.

I left the marsh marigolds and continued up the creek, and to my delight found rapids sparkling in the sunlight, with the small new leaves of an alderbush silhouetted against them. Nearby on a warm sunny bank under a stand of aspen were the first mayflowers, some of them white and others a deep and startling blue. Beside them, close to the water's edge, were a single clump of blue violets and the nodding green heads of the dogtooth bursting out of the brown leaves.

On a flat surface of black mud grew a stand of horsetail or equisetum, so called because the delicate and feathery stems look like the tail of a horse. Behind them and closer to the drier bank the fiddleheads of ferns had pushed through the muck, the round, smoothly curving tips resembling the end of a violin. On the bank above them both was a dense mat of princess pine two or three inches tall—one of the club mosses known as lycopodium. All spore-producers, these plants existed long before flowering plants evolved.

Now tiny and dwarfed, they are all that is left of the forested swamps of the Mesozoic era several hundred million years ago. This was truly the forest primeval, with tree ferns, lycopodia, and equisetum three or four feet in diameter and a hundred feet or more in height, a dense tropical jungle, the home of huge Amphibia and enormous dinosaurs, the birthplace of mammals and birds and eventually of the forerunners of man. It was a carboniferous period, when great beds of coal and deposits of oil and gas, the basic sources of energy for our industrial civilization, were laid down. In New York a flash flood raced out of the Catskills one spring a century ago, uncovering petrified stumps of tree ferns standing exactly where they had died when the swamps disappeared and were covered with silt. Coal beds today show beautiful fossils of ferns and bark, of stumps and leaves.

I picked a stem of princess pine and studied the club at its tip, which had borne a cloud of golden spores the season before. The little plant was no different from what it used to be; it varied only in size. Nor had the ferns beside it changed, for they showed the very same fronds as graced the tall trees of old. It was fitting that they should emerge together during the time of flowers to remind us of the vast expanses of time, the eons of evolution before the colorful blossoms of spring came into being.

By mid-May the arbutus were in bloom on a sunny bank beneath the jack pines. I cupped a cluster of the newly opened buds in my hand and sniffed the most delicate odor of all, the first intimations of warming earth and surging life. Then one bright morning when the robins were caroling and the silvery notes of the whitethroats sounded everywhere, the entire hillside was in bloom. Between the clumps were blueberries in blossom, and countless plants of Canadian mayflower pushed their single spadelike leaves through the needles. The long, cold months, the smooth whiteness, the shadows, the tracks in the snow, and the frigid winds out of the north were over.

Spring merged into summer with the fading of the marigolds, trilliums, and arbutus. Hepatica leaves grew large and lay flat against the ground. The pink lady-slippers, once bold and showy, their roots kept cool by sphagnum, were now gone, as were the rosy blossoms of polygala from under the pines, the delicate greenish white of pyrolas, pipsissewa, and the golden sprays of clintonia.

Wild flowers, though they play a vital role in the design of the forest floor, play an equally important role in the joy of those who find them.

A DRIFT OF POLLEN

The little bay was rimmed with a strange translucent light, and the shore, the rocks, the windfalls, and the sand along the beach seemed tinted with new gold. It was pollen time, and the entire forest reflected the glow. It was the end of flowering for millions of herbs, shrubs, and trees. The long pendant catkins of alder, birch, and aspen, the purple and crimson rosettes of the staminate blossoms of pines, all had shed their burden and in the process fertilized waiting ovules that would now begin the growth of seeds. The pollen produced in such extravagant profusion had drifted over lakes and pools and through the forest everywhere, down into the most inaccessible places, filtering its golden horde into every hidden crevice. Tiny cones would now begin to take shape but would not mature for another year.

I picked up a pebble painted with the gold and examined the shape and structure of the pollen with a magnifying glass. The grains had many shapes, most of them round or oval, with definite markings, striations, and stipplings. An almost indestructible protein, resistant to decay, the pollen grains can retain their identity for thousands of years. When they settle into the waters of a lake or bog, they eventually sink to the bottom to mix with the decayed vegetation or peat, and remain there unchanged in a stable environment, safe from erosion by the elements.

Once I made a survey of the bogs of the area with a famous paleobotanist and saw through his eyes the pollen grains embedded there. He bored down into the packed muddy bottoms of many bogs and brought up cores of layered peat from as deep as twenty to thirty feet; from them he could tell the age of the layer at any depth and identify the pollen grains. Knowing that each plant has a distinctive pollen type, he had an infallible key to the phantom forests of the past and to all the species that composed them.

The first layers produced after the glacier's retreat some ten thousand years ago contained the pollen of spruce and fir, indicating a cold, wet climate. Then came an invasion of jack pine, meaning a drier and somewhat warmer era—a change, however, that took several thousand years. Above the jack pine, the pollen of red and white pine was mixed with the rest, telling of a still milder period. When maples, birches, and aspen came into the profile with the conifers, the climate was no doubt somewhat similar to our own. By using the radioactivity of carbon as a time scale, the paleobotanist found it took from 500 to 1000 years to form a foot of peat, and that some of the bogs were 25,000 years or more in age.

Phantom forests succeeding one another over the centuries told not only of changes in climate, but of cataclysmic events that occurred long before the coming of man. Great fires caused by lightning swept over the land 3500 years ago, leaving their black charcoal in the peat. Numerous other conflagrations also left their traces, but none were holocausts of the violence and enormous extent of the first.

To paleobotanists, the tale of the pollen grains is a dramatic one of advancing and retreating glaciers, of depressions gouged out of solid rock by enormous masses of ice, of disturbed drainages caused by the deposition of morainic debris, of hidden blocks of ice whose final melting produced deep ponds. They tell of flood periods that came with warming temperatures, of swollen rivers, enormous lakes, and literally millions of ponds, and of the first drifting into them of glacial silts and windblown dust from the grinding down of rock, which formed the base of soils for the forests to come. Here there was even evidence of pollen grains carried over long distances from the south. They told how the glacial ponds became ringed with mosses, lichens, and heathers even before the coming of the trees, and how at last the ponds were closed by the vegetation encroaching upon them.

This was just another spring in the long history of the forests. For thousands of years before I came, the shores had been just as golden, the pollen grains dusting the surface of the land as they always had during the spring. Should another ice age come with bitter cold and the grinding weight of a glacier, the forests about me would disappear again and all forms of life vanish, setting the stage once more. I looked at the pines, the cedars and balsams, the aspen and birch, at the gay flowers blooming everywhere. Some day in the far distant future, men might come again to study the bogs, reconstructing from pollen grains the phantom forest that stood around me now.

WINGS AGAINST THE MOON

I could hear the geese high overhead, the glorious gabbling only they can achieve, a sound that seems to hold all the wild freedom of the wilderness, of continental expanses, of the unseen and unknown of far places. I could not see them, but as they circled they were close enough so I could hear the whistle of their wings. The moon was full, and I hoped to catch them against its light. Then it happened: first a single bird was etched in black, then two or three, and finally the entire flock streamed in silhouette against the yellow glowing surface. The geese were on their way north, would fly until they found ice, and rest there while the sun melted the bogs, creeks, and lakes of their nesting areas along the southern reaches of Hudson Bay.

One single glimpse was all I had, but it was enough. Now I could hear the gabbling growing fainter and fainter in the distance, and then it was swallowed by the dark. Later, when the moon was high, there was a constant calling far above: shorebirds, sparrows, warblers, songbirds of all kinds, until there seemed no end. All these were on their way, and as I listened I tried to catch some meaning from the music, some hint of the mystery of migration in the spring and fall, but no answers came, no wisdom distilled from years of wondering, only the thrill of knowing the birds were moving once more, and the joy of being there as they went over.

Birds do not always wait for moonlight or clear skies, but often travel when the earth is shrouded with clouds and mist. Sometimes I think they prefer stormy weather, and, as always, I wonder how they find their way, on what compass they depend for their unfailing sense of direction. Do they follow magnetic lines of force? Do cosmic rays influence them, or the spinning of the earth? Have they some subtle continental sense, some built-in terrestrial map that tells them where to go? Do prevailing winds and air currents high above the earth serve them, as they do ships at sea? No one knows exactly what the answers are, and possibly no one ever will, but this we know, that, in spite of the homing instinct, birds get lost and are not infallible but are subject to lack of judgment as all living creatures are. The lost ones fail to add their inheritance to the genetic pool of the race, which is just as well, for only those strong enough to survive pass on their experience.

In the morning I saw many new arrivals, different kinds of sparrows: song sparrows, chipping sparrows, and even some Harris males with their black vests and dignified stance. Warblers were high in the trees, darting and flashing everywhere, and along the edge of a pool, on a little mudflat, a flock of sandpipers dipped and weaved as they searched for food.

In one end of a swampy bay were two mallards, the male, a beautiful greenhead, glistening in the sunlight, while the demure female investigated the rushes for a possible nesting site. A pair of loons were out on the open water, and I heard their laughing for the first time that spring. The chickadees, who had been there all winter, seemed excited by the invasion of strangers, and their mating calls were loud and clear. All were stirred by that strange hormonic triggering that told them the time had come. This calling as birds fly over the earth is a sign of spring as important as the swelling of buds or the sound of running water. Almost any night you can hear them, and men always will, if we cherish and do not destroy the earth.

PAGES 25-36

25. A Cape May warbler, fresh from the south, matches the golden budding willows of a bog.

26-27. A tracery of maple leaves bursts forth, rosy and shining, against gray-green lichen-covered ledges.

28. As the black muck of a stream bank is warmed by the spring sun, fiddleheads of ferns all but explode toward the light.

29. A spotted ladybug blends in almost perfect camouflage with the lichens on the bark of a dead aspen.

30. The bobcat, all eyes and sensitive awareness, alert to sounds that might promise food, is always ready to begin a gliding stalk as smooth and quiet as the surrounding shadows.

31. Rivulets of melted snow, bordered by delicate gardens of ferns, mosses, and spring flowers, tumble over rocks and ledges in a lacework of glistening white.

32-33. The wing feather of a bluejay, bright against the brown of snow-packed leaves, is a mute reminder of the foray of some hawk or owl.

34-35. Emerging leaves of large-leaved asters, dwarf dogwood, and anemonies will soon hide a small moose antler.

36. Violets growing close to the water's edge.

SUMMER

A CERTAIN FULLNESS

When a poet said, "What is so rare as a day in June?" he knew whereof he spoke. In spite of rain, black flies, and mosquitoes, when the sun does shine in June, it means that summer is here at last. While only two months have passed since the ice went out, the snow disappeared from the valleys into plunging rivers and creeks full to the brim, and the skies were alive with multitudes of songbirds returning from the south, when such a day comes, it is as though it had always been warm and bright, so short is memory and the dream of a millennium.

June is the time of transition between spring and the fullness of summer. The pastel variations of foliage have settled into dark and full-blown greens, early blossoms have faded, the stippled white of dwarf dogwood is on the ground, the snowy drifts of plum and cherry are on the hillsides. The twinflower or Linnaea is pink beneath the pines, and the gold of the bead lily shows among the birches. Lady-slippers stand shy and tremulous above the cushioned sphagnum in the low places. Flood waters are subsiding, creeks and rivers resuming their normal steady flow. The weather is no longer temperamental, but calm and predictable, as though the season had at long last decided what it will be.

June belongs to the young. The birds that arrived in such a gay flurry after the breakup have long since finished their mating and nest-building. Downy fledglings clamor open-mouthed for food. Spotted fawns are finding their legs, young squirrels peek wide-eyed at the magical world of treetops, coveys of partridge chicks are learning to hide under last year's leaves. Tight little rafts of ducklings follow their mothers along the shorelines, darting swiftly into the cover of sedges and brush at the approach of danger. The red-winged blackbirds, still balancing on the reeds, sing their hearts out all day long, but there is something missing now, the note of fierce challenge to all comers that dominated them when they first chose their nesting sites. Loons still call, but they are through with wild displays of courtship and the strange cavortings over the breeding bays where they nested.

By mid-July, foliage is heavy under summer showers. Berries are ripening on the forest floor: greenish-yellow clusters of dogwood, partridgeberry, bearberry. Strawberries are through bearing, but raspberries are coming into their own. Covered with the dews of morning, they glow with an almost translucent light. Pincherries, chokecherries, and Indian plums are swelling and showing hints of red. Blueberries are ripening, and in places where the sun has touched them there is already a wash of powder-blue. Birds, squirrels, mice, and bears gorge themselves on the harvest.

The air is alive over lakes and ponds and in the woods themselves—midges, caddis flies, and mayflies—and at dusk there is a hum of millions of wings until it seems as though this were an insect world. Rising fish dimple the waters. Bass are off their spawning beds, wall-eyed pike cruise over reefs and rocky points, and great northerns, those tigers of shallow bays, lie in wait in ambush jungles of rushes and water weeds. Swallows and nighthawks swoop and soar, gleaning from the surfaces of water, slicing through the misty swarms of insects, clouds of them lifting from earth and among the trees.

During August, the northern forest is bursting with so many forms of life, it seems impossible it can contain them all. After a warm summer rain, when the forest floor is all but steaming with an almost tropical beauty, there is a feeling of unlimited life, an awareness of forms growing everywhere in places which a short time before seemed barren. It is then that billions of spores suddenly find conditions right for growth, and with speed and unbelievable variety fungi, lichens, mosses, and ferns magically appear. There is little green among the fungi, but every other hue of the spectrum: reds and oranges, purples and yellows, blacks and whitish pinks, and unimaginable and infinite variations. On logs and on the bark of trees grow shelf fungi, strange horizontal growths with convoluted edges, but it is on the floor itself that most of the growth takes place: mushrooms of all kinds, from tiny growths of perhaps a quarter of an inch in height to enormous ones of a foot in diameter. Not all are mushroom-shaped; some protruding from the duff are like tiny yellow candles, perfect stalks of miniature coral, or round little balls.

Along the forest edges, in open grassy places away from the shade of trees, grow fairy rings of demure pearl-white-colored caps, always in a circle beginning from a single spore in the very center of the ring. Fungi epitomize summer's unlimited wealth, the lavish abandonment with which nature assures life's continuance by producing far more sperms and eggs, spores and seeds than can ever mature. Living on decaying vegetation, unable to make food by means of chlorophyll like other plants, they survive on the largesse of those who do.

As August wanes, our old forgotten sense of urgency awakens once more as we realize summer may actually be as short as spring. Sunshine, warmth, and the long days must not be wasted. It is a temptation to lie in the sun during the day and stay awake half the night, watching sunsets, moonrises, and northern lights, listening to the calling of the loons, or watching some storm with its jagged shafts of lightning between rising thunderheads. It is almost a pity to miss a single sunrise or the mists of early morning over meadows and valleys. There is so much to feel and see, the days and nights are never long enough. There is no waiting for tomorrow, for tomorrow may never come.

Summer means promises fulfilled, objectives gained, hopes realized. The surge of doing and achieving, of watching and enjoying is finally replaced by a sense of quiet and floating and a certain fullness and repletion, as though one cannot absorb any more. Then one day, lying on a path, there is a tiny leaf of aspen, bright yellow with a border of red along the veins. This is a sign, and I look at it with disbelief. It cannot be true. It is far too early, for the dark green and the fullness is still around, with growth moving swiftly as ever. My eyes refuse to accept what they have seen, but memory overrules. I pick up the leaf and twirl it between my fingers, then lay it back again on the trail.

THE PINE STUMP

Caribou Creek has its source in a bog of sphagnum moss and heather. In the spring its black pools are bright with marsh marigolds and the crimson of blossoming tamarack. In the summer blue and white violets bloom along its edges, and in the fall, when the ash trees turn lemon-yellow and the tamaracks to smoky gold, the pools are dusted with their sheen.

Around the bog is a gravel ridge on which once grew red and white pines. Ten thousand years ago, when the continental glacier began its retreat, a great block of ice settled and, when it melted, left the hollow of the bog. For centuries a pond was there, but in time it became covered with vegetation. Through the bog ran trickles from springs and seepages which gathered themselves together and escaped toward the lake a mile below. The beavers built a dam across the creek, and it spread out into a placid pool, where in the early days hunters waited for caribou to come and drink.

The bog is still there, but the big pines around it are gone; only the old stumps remain. Some still show gray and weathered wood, but most are covered with mosses and plants that have taken root. All of them are going into decay, and each speaks of the past and the glories it has known.

First settlers told me how the pines looked in the early days, when the town below was a rough mining camp hewn out of the woods: how tall and straight the trees were, so close that the sunlight barely filtered through to the deep layer of needles and duff below.

Before me is one of the largest stumps, fully five feet across the butt. Part is still hard, the rest green and soft in its mossy covering. It is as though the bog itself were reaching up to reclaim what is left of the tree. In that green, invading tongue of moss is a patch of wintergreen with bright red berries and waxen leaves. At its base is a log covered with the vines of partridgeberry, and on the lower side a luxuriant stand of ground pine with erect yellow stalks of spores trailing down the slope.

Several orange fungi have taken root in the log, as well as a clump of dwarf dogwood with white four-petaled flowers. In the fall the red berries of dogwood, partridgeberry, and wintergreen will provide a feast for the grouse and migrant songbirds coming through.

The vines of Linnaea and cranberry are woven through the network, and at one point a striped maple is struggling to get its share of the sun. The log and stump are crowded with plants: gold thread, windflowers, a stalk of Labrador tea, and several grasses and sedges, in a complex interweaving of one into the other to form a mat that not only protects the shallow bed of humus from erosion, but holds the moisture for a while before it trickles down into the reservoir of the swamp.

The pine stump with the log beside it is the story of old age and the passing into the forest floor of a great tree, but in the bright new colors, the verdant green and richness of many plants growing upon it, is the story of rebirth. These are reminders that the forest means change and succession, and that there is no permanence except in the stream of life itself. This is the pattern of the future, a symbol of the design for all living things on earth.

THE BOULDER

The boulder lay alone beneath the jack pines. It was water-worn and rounded by the surging rapids of some ancient river. The great glacier moving south from Hudson Bay had plucked it from the riverbed and carried it to its present resting place. When the ice finally melted, it was left on a barren moraine of sand and gravel overlying the naked rock of the Canadian Shield.

Then there was no forest floor, for there were no plants nor any soil for their growth. But that was long ago, and now the boulder is surrounded by a cushion of dark earth from millennia of weathering and decay. Over this humus is a layer of pine needles and duff.

The boulder is covered with lichens, the most primitive and widely spread land plants on earth. They grow on rocks, on the bark of trees, and on the ground itself. Hundreds of millions of years before other forms came into being, they thrived and eventually evolved into what they are today, a combination of fungi and algae. The two forms of life originally lived apart until, perhaps, some exploring thread of fungus may have encircled and held in its grasp a single cell of alga, creating a combination never known before, the beginning of an ancient plant ownership. The fungus, through its acid-exuding rootlets, absorbed food materials from naked rock, the alga with its chloroplasts produced starch out of sunshine and air. Because of the cooperative arrangement, lichens survived where many other plants died.

Some of these strange plants look like gray and brittle paint; others grow in light green circular patterns or resemble black and crusted leaves. They grow slowly, and some patches no more than an inch or two in diameter may be as old as fifty years. After the glacial retreat, when all the land was barren and devoid of life, billions of spores drifted in on southerly winds, covering not only the boulder itself but the gravel around it and the ledge on which it lay. Many were caught on the rocks' rough surfaces and, with moisture and warmth, burst into life. Slowly the probing holdfasts worked their way down into the rock, gradually widening tiny fissures, and when water seeped in, followed by frost, the cracks opened still farther. As these first plants decayed, humus was formed, preparing a bed for the seeds of flowers. At last, even in the cracks of the ledge beneath, there was enough soil for trees, for aspen, birch, and maple, for spruce, balsam, and pine. But the lichens were everywhere—patches and tufts of caribou moss, tiny red spore cups on logs and stumps and on the bark of dead and living trees, clusters of orange, russet, and yellow.

For a long time there was no change, until after a summer storm and lightning, when fire engulfed the ledge and the tight cones on a few old jack pines burst their bonds and seeded the area all around. Now the boulder lay as before beneath a dense stand of trees. It had been part of it all, the unfolding of the master plan.

On the shady side is a growth called rock tripe—*tripe du roche* the French Voyageurs named it—because of its resemblance on the underside to cows' tripe, a common food in Europe. When boiled, this lichen provides nourishment, and many a wilderness traveler has used it when faced with starvation. When dry, it is brittle and almost black; when wet by the rains, it softens and turns olive green.

Perched on the very top of the rock is a small cluster of caribou moss, which looks like a silvery leafless shrub only an inch or two in height. Found all over the north and far into the Arctic with such plants as willow and dwarf birch, it is the major food of caribou.

On a decayed stub is a clump of painted lichen, the cap of each stalk a brilliant vermilion. Indians believed the Little People colored it as a prank to make this lowly form more beautiful than the rest. Nearby are some lichens with tiny cups filled with dew. The variety seems infinite, and they all have the same ability to flourish and survive.

I discover rock fern that has taken root in a deep fissure. Its roots, I know, go far into the granite, holding firmly against the winds which threaten it. The plant is compact and firmly set; the undersides of the fronds are brown with spores. It will stay until the boulder disintegrates.

Just beyond the boulder, in a dip in the ground where leaves and humus are deep, is a stand of rare Indian pipe, its hue an off-white. Five ghostly stalks of it have pushed up through the needles, each with a curved and drooping head. A seed-bearing plant, it has no chlorophyll or the slightest hint of green, but must depend for sustenance on the products of decay of other plants.

Toward the edge of the jack-pine knoll, where sunlight shines in the afternoons, is a patch of blueberries, fully ripe. The bears would like to find them, feast, and scatter their seeds. Birds and squirrels may find them too, but as yet the berries are untouched and waiting—I think, for me. I kneel and pick a handful and fill my hat, and think of the spring and the pinkish cups of the flowers at the time the Linnaea bloomed.

On the north side of the knoll mosses have grown, huge clumps of them, like enormous pincushions. Tightly grown, they indicate water seepage beneath, and, as though to prove it, there is a stand of black spruce which might have been part of the swamp below.

This is the world of the boulder, and all growth has come since the barren arctic era of the glacier's retreat. It is symbolic of the past and of the north, where primitive plants must struggle for survival in a harsh environment. Sitting there beneath the sheltering jack pines, it is a reminder to harried men of the slow passage of time.

Some day the boulder will crumble, and already there are widening telltale fissures. During a future winter when they are filled with ice, the frost will force the boulder apart. In time it may disintegrate completely and will then add richness to the soil and provide even more places for plants to grow.

A SHAFT OF SUNLIGHT

High in the tops of the pine trees was a new opening where the sun came through in a shaft reaching down to the forest floor. Until the great pine had fallen, that opening was closed, the entire floor bathed in continuous shadow. Now the light came through for the first time since the canopy had formed, and I wondered what it would mean. Sunlight is the great determinant in a forest, deciding which plants will grow and which will die.

There are two kinds of trees, the tolerant ones that will grow in shade, and the intolerant, which will not. In between are innumerable variations and compromises, until it is difficult to place any plant in a definite category because of other influences such as moisture, humidity, and soil, which affect the all-pervading impact of light. Pines are intolerant and must have the sun to live, but even they vary in their needs. Red pines, more affected by shade than others, lose their lower branches early, and as a result their trunks are tall and smooth almost to the top. White pines, with more tolerance, keep their lower branches longer, and their boles are not quite as clean.

Maples and oaks, aspen and birch, balsam and spruce are tolerant of shade and will survive beneath pines, but when the big trees fall to the ground, these waiting species reach for the sun and grow swiftly in its light. Seldom do all the pines die at once, except in a great fire or windstorm, so the new forest in all probability becomes a mixture of both types.

I walked through the woods to see what had happened in other places and found a spot where another pine had fallen years before and several pines had taken root in the exposed soil at its base. The seedlings were tall, but might grow to ten or twenty feet without more than a tuft of branches near the tip. A balsam had started beside them. It too was reaching for the light, but with more branches than the pines, enough to shade and kill the young saplings unless their growth was swift enough to keep them high and safe from its competition.

A maple was also there, and, to one side, a tiny birch. A cluster of dwarf dogwood was growing beside the stump, and a thin stem of blueberry. The top of the log was covered with mosses, lichens, tiny ferns, and many other plants, among them feathery spruces.

As I looked at all these young plants, I wondered which would win the race, if the opening high above would stay without change. The branches of neighboring pines were already moving toward the space where the light came through, responding like all the rest to the great bonanza of sunlight. If the tops should close too tightly, they could seal the doom of the plants below.

That shaft of sunlight was a precious thing, of far greater importance to all species involved than the return of a great tree to the soil. It was an indicator of what could happen should all the pines fall and sunlight drench the places where they had grown, warming the soil and stimulating unseen forms of life. There would be many changes, not only in the character of the forest itself but in all creatures dependent upon it. Squirrels would move out to other stands of cone-producing trees, followed by the martens and owls, and by nuthatches seeking the pines they need. While the new deciduous growth was young, deer would come in to feed on the tender browse, and with them rabbits, partridge, and whitefooted mice. Vireos, thrushes, and sparrows would frequent the vibrant new forest and keep it alive with song. Foxes and weasels, hawks and owls would soon return, and the old pine forest with its sighing tops and silences would be forgotten.

As the aspen matured and grew old, the pileated woodpeckers would move in to harvest the grubs and dig great holes in the soft wood for their nesting. With the creation of this new canopy of shade, young plants would become scarcer, and once more animals of the forest floor would be forced to move into the sunlight that determines where they can live and survive.

PAGES 49-72

49. The red fox is one of the most beautiful of the predators that help to maintain the ecological balance of the forest.

50-51. A pine log slowly sinking into the forest floor, thickly grown with vines and flowering plants, with lush lichens and mosses, and with tiny trees, is a veritable nursery to a host of growing things.

52-53. The dappled colors of a spotted fawn offer little protection beside an open lake.

54. Rain and mist drain down the veins of leaves and gather at every point to form glistening jewels shining in brief glory until the sun takes them all away.

55. The strange powers of surface stress and tension scatter drops of moisture like evenly spaced pearls along the slender strands of a spiderweb.

56-57. Stalks of Indian pipe emerge ghostlike from the rich humus and mosses beneath the spruces.

58. The bog itself seems to be reaching up to reclaim a great broken stump of pine, all that is left of a mighty tree felled by some windstorm of the past.

59. The raccoon, a hunter of the night, is extending its range into the pine forest of the north.

60-61. After a rain, the forest floor really blooms as millions of spores of fungi, mosses, and mushrooms spring to life in unimaginable and infinite variations of color.

62. In places where the sun has touched the blueberries with its magic, there is already a wash of powder-blue.

63. The *hoo-hoo-hoo-hooooooo* of a great horned owl is a warning for all small living things to be still, for its soundless wings in the dusk could bring death.

64-65. Lichens grow on the rough surfaces of boulders and rock ledges, and in the crevices where humus has gathered, young trees and ferns take root, as part of the forces that eventually bring rock down to earth.

66. A shady north slope with water trickling underneath supports deep beds of cushioned moss, acid soil, and stands of small but ancient spruce.

67. The red squirrel is the busiest food-gatherer of the forest, perhaps the happiest, and surely the noisiest and most exuberant.

68-69. The hairy wheatlike capsules of pigeon-wheat moss will soon open, and as the wind shakes the slender threadlike stalks, the spores will take to the air.

70-71. A summer sunset displays black silhouettes against the horizon, flame-red waters, and mallards gathering for the great migration southward.

72. The golden fruiting cups of lichens form a painted garden on the decaying bark of an aspen.

AUTUMN

BANNERS AGAINST THE SKY

It was a morning in late August, and the air had a certain crispness about it which had not been there before, a feeling entirely different from summer's balminess, an unmistakable hint of fall. Then, as though to prove without question that things had changed far beyond the first telltale colors in single leaves, before me on a rocky point was a branch of maple flaming against the sky.

That red had always been there, though hidden by the green of chlorophyll, not showing until the advent of frost or lack of moisture. For some reason that single branch had changed, while the rest of the tree was solid green. Perhaps the wind had caught it, twisting the stem and choking off the normal flow of sap. Possibly an insect, a bird, or a squirrel had gnawed through the long supply tubules in the living cambium beneath the bark. Whatever the reason, that first exciting touch of color was a promise of riotous weeks to come when the whole north would be not only aflame but electric with an excitement that touched all living things.

Autumn begins with little events such as this, a single leaf or branch, or a barely perceptible tinge of yellow in a stand of ash in some quiet bay or swamp or in a grove of white birches on a hillside. And this is perhaps as it should be, for if it came all at once it would be hard for color-sensitive human beings to endure. Autumn is more than the flamboyance of reds and yellows. It is a change in a way of life, a getting ready for the icy winds of the north.

Some time later, on a portage over a barren rocky slope, I saw a cluster of sumac, a scarlet whorl of leaves. Looking down into its center was like gazing into a whirlpool of red, with the deepest shade in its very heart. As I carried my canoe, I caught glimpses of the rapids and a branch of birch, bright yellow against the sparkling blue and white of the water. And at the end where the river turned, a scarlet woodbine twined around a gray and weathered stub.

The grasses, ferns, and bracken along the shore were turning to bronze, and carpets of crimson berries covered the ground on sunny slopes. A little swamp was turning to copper, and cranberries lay like rubies against the moss.

A month later the shores of all the lakes had turned to red and gold, and on one quiet afternoon it seemed as though the islands were floating in a haze of color. Points of rock lay like giant spears on the surface, and at a distance it was hard to tell where shorelines began and ended, so completely fused were the reflections—blue and gold, bronze and yellow, red and mahogany, with infinite variations in between. A madness had seized the land, as though a painter in wild desperation had squandered his whole palette in a grand orgy of exaltation.

A week after, I stood beneath a great aspen whose gold stood boldly against the sky. The leaves began to flutter, and then came the wind; in an instant the air was alive with a cascade of drifting leaves. The ground was soon deep with them, and now I could look far into the woods and see what had happened to the forest floor itself. Cherry bushes had turned to wine, mountain maple to peach and rose, hazel to rusty gold, and small shrubs and herbs to combinations of them all—a kaleidoscope of shifting shades that until then had been hidden from view except along the fringes of the trees. These colors were more delicate than the rest, having been protected from wind and direct sunlight.

Soon even this final color was gone, when even the scrub oaks on barren hilltops began to lose their hard-won banners to the gales. The wild rice in bays and rivermouths was still golden, but fading with the rest. Ice formed over ponds and in sheltered pools, and the earth froze hard at night. Trees were now bare traceries against the sky, and leaden clouds hung low.

One cold, gray afternoon rich with the smells of wet and molding leaves, the air was suddenly full of drifting flakes of snow, and I watched with amazement as though I had never seen them before. They settled on a tuft of painted lichen, on a cluster of mountain-ash berries still bright red, and on the fading bronzes of sarsaparilla, coating the last of autumn's beauty with a filigree of silver that disappeared as swiftly as it came. Some of the flakes stayed on a leaf of sumac in a sheltered corner between the rocks, and there was a dusting on the gray-green of lichen and on a shelf of bright orange fungus on a log.

That day I found a quiet ice-rimmed pool where the leaves on the bottom, responding to the movement of water, drifted in a shifting panorama of color. Round and round they moved, constantly changing position, still as brilliant as when they fell. While I watched, the ground was speckled with white, and I was conscious of an almost inaudible whispering as more and more snow came down. Within an hour the earth was sealed and white.

FIRE SCAR

Most trees have scars upon them. Marks of experience, they are evidence of the trees' survival in spite of injuries. Some scars never heal; others are hidden by new tissues growing over and around them, but even so, they often deform and change growth patterns. All of them, no matter what their cause, are wound stripes in a sense, bringing in their train a host of influences both good and bad, and often initiating natural successions in vegetational growth of benefit to the environment and to all living things dependent upon it.

In forests there are many kinds of scars: places where branches have been broken by wind or heavy snows, or gnawed by porcupines, beaver, mice, and rabbits, or by larger animals such as moose, caribou, or deer. Where tips have been killed by sunscald or freezing, where gallflies have laid their eggs in the buds of willow or oak, or where fungi have taken hold in the living layers of cambium, we find scars resembling flower-like growths on willow, or the dense bushy masses on spruce known as witches'-brooms. The reasons are many, the results oftentimes bizarre, but even though wounds may almost disappear, there is usually some telltale mark the tree or shrub carries during its lifetime.

Around me were tall pines, some two hundred years or more in age, towering toward the sky, the brown forest floor almost in twilight beneath them. Many had prominent fire scars, cat-faces they call them in the north, charred areas extending from the ground several feet up the trunk. Few had escaped the burn of possibly half a century before, the trees carrying their evidence until they toppled to the earth. Fire scars—the result of tragedy? No, simply proof of an ecological force as inevitable in the north as the coming of the seasons, of snow and cold, of drought and rain, a force that determines vegetational types, trees and shrubs, flowers and grasses, mosses, lichens and ferns, and all animal life as well. The north has been shaped by fire for untold thousands of years; fire scars are merely reminders of what has taken place many times.

Beneath the pines the needle-strewn floor was clean and unbroken. Few plants grew between them—occasionally a clump of blueberry, the thin stem of a starflower, a cluster of fern, or a bit of gray lichen on a protruding stone. On an old log, soft and spongy with decay, grew mosses interlaced with the vines of Linnaea and partridgeberry. Several seedlings had taken root on it, a birch, a balsam, and a delicate feathery spruce. There were no young pines.

I lay down on the resilient layer of needles and looked up into the canopy above. The air was never still: needles drifted down, whirling, spinning like little tops; tiny scales of bark, gossamer spiderwebs moved with them. Bits of branches floated down too, adding to the debris already there, the two or three inches that had accumulated since the pines began to grow. This constant shower of debris from the great trees has a purpose as important as rain itself, the building up of a layer of duff that eventually becomes humus.

I dug into the dry crisscrossed layer of needles. Rust-red in color at the surface, it became darker as I went down, and turned almost black as it approached the area of decay or humus. Now I could feel the moisture, and I dug down two inches, four, and finally six before I came to the light mineral soil, the result of erosion of the bedrock itself.

A squirrel scurried down one of the pines, stopped on a branch just above, and watched me suspiciously, stomping its feet and chattering with alarm. Satisfied that there was no real danger, it jumped to the ground with a pine cone in its teeth. It investigated a dozen places, finally chose one, and dug a hole into the brown duff so deep only its tail protruded. Emerging, it covered the opening to its precious store, ran swiftly back to the pine and once again into the high cone-bearing branches. Sometime during the winter, if the snow is not too deep, it will hunt for that cone, and perhaps actually find it. In the spring, if conditions are right, the seeds within the cone might sprout and a pine take root.

On such a forest floor beneath the pines, few seeds ever germinate because of the dryness of the layer of needles and the slight chance any of them has of coming in contact with moisture, humus, or even mineral soil. If one pine germinates from a hundred or a thousand cones, it is a miracle, for dryness and the killing shade are the great eliminators.

A pine had taken root in soil exposed where a tree had fallen. It was very spindly, reaching toward an opening high above where a single ray of sunshine came through at noon. It had a chance of survival, provided its neighbors did not close the gap too soon. Only time would tell whether the seedling would replace the pine which first gave it a chance.

The layer of humus beneath the duff is the result of thousands of years of decay. Here is the real wealth of the forest, for it is literally alive with countless microscopic forms of life which change dead material, through the chemistry of decay, to nutrients used by the living. Through it go the exploring rootlets of trees, the burrows of worms and insects, of mice and squirrels, all of them letting in air and moisture and giving it the friability and texture necessary for healthy growth. Its water-holding capacity is phenomenal. Sand will hold a quarter of its weight in water; clay, one half; humus, the black gold of the forest, twice its weight, making it the greatest reservoir of the land. The tawny duff is dead and dry, merely a warm insulating layer protecting the humus from erosion and providing shelter for the many busy lives thriving within it.

When a wildfire sweeps through a forest, a violent blaze burning through logging slash, across areas leveled by windstorm or disease or by man's unwise interference with normal cycles, humus is the real loss. I reached down into the hole I had dug through the loose dry duff, deep into the humus itself, and brought up a handful. It smelled rich and clean, and when I crumbled it in my hand, it did not stick to my fingers. Here was the elemental fertility of the continent, holding within it the trace elements and such major sources of food as nitrogen, phosphorus, and calcium—everything needed for growth. It was unchanged and unpolluted by insecticides or herbicides, and creatures feeding upon the plants it produced would be strong and vital. The duff was the humus to come, fertility in the making. Humus gave height to the pines, brilliance to flowers, fullness to fruit, and viability to seeds. It alone was responsible for the sheen of fur and feathers, for the glisten of leaves and the song of birds. Here was the basis of life itself.

The black fire scars on the pines around me spoke of fires that had not destroyed humus and duff, fires burning slowly along the surface of the ground, killing most of the young plants, it is true, but allowing the trees to survive. By so doing, fires actually kept the pines safe from the violence of tremendous conflagrations which might have destroyed them before they were mature.

They reminded me of the far north, where, looking over many miles of terrain and rolling ridges with broad valleys in between them and waterways fading into the distance, one sees the everlasting pattern of fire, the great fire scars of the past. Recent burns are covered with the reddish-purple blaze of fireweed, those slightly older with the light green of aspen and birch, those older still with the somewhat darker shade of scattered spruce and pine coming in, and finally, the oldest of all by the dark green of solid coniferous growth.

The entire land, all vegetation and animal life, has adapted itself to constant and recurring change. When fires have swept across it, tender new shoots of aspen, birch, and willow spring up by the millions, forging new food chains for rabbits, mice, and birds, which in turn are preyed upon by bobcats, lynx, foxes and weasels, predatory hawks and owls. Moose, deer, and caribou also benefit by the increase in new browse, and the wolves that prey upon them respond like all other forms to the surge of new life following fires.

Without the changes fire brings in its wake, great areas might become sterile deserts devoid of food, with mature stands such as the pines predominating. In the tops I could hear the nasal *hank-hank-hank* of the nuthatches and the chattering of the squirrel; in the background, the great and ancient silence and the soft moaning of the wind in the high branches.

I walked through the grove to its edge, where the logging had stopped some twenty years before. Here were young aspen and birch with an occasional balsam and a ground cover of striped maple, honeysuckle, and bracken fern. I listened to the violin notes of a hermit thrush, the flutelike call of a white-throated sparrow, the *teacher-teacher* of an ovenbird. Following one of the logging roads almost hidden with grass and clover, I flushed a partridge with a flock of well-grown chicks. A deer had walked across the trail, and I found the pellet of a great horned owl. Here was food, abundant food—berries, buds, worms, insects, and mice—and this was a place for living things.

On a dry rocky ridge toward one side of the logging was a solid stand of jack pine growing so thickly there was room for nothing else. Here the flames of a lightning fire, spurred on perhaps by the logging's aftermath of debris, had been hot enough to explode the tight cones on a few old jacks, and the winged seeds were blown everywhere by the hot, furious winds. Because some of the duff had burned, humus and even mineral soil were exposed, and the seeds germinated by the thousands, to grow into the jungle before me. This was the habitat of Kirtland's warbler, which has possibly the most restricted range of any bird. It thrives only in young, bushy stands of jack pine from three to fifteen feet high, in such places as central Michigan, feeding on the insects it finds there, and always wintering in the Bahamas. As soon as the pines grow too large and sparse, it must move in search of younger trees, so specialized has this little warbler become.

Fire shapes environments for many creatures, but it also plays a role as a cleanser and purifier, destroying insects, larvae, and disease whenever they become so virulent as to threaten survival. Such scourges are often the result of overcrowding and lack of free circulation of air and water. The budworm, sweeping over millions of acres of balsam and spruce, leaves vast jungles of dead entangled trees inviting borers and insects of all kinds, which result finally in pestilential areas of great danger to all life.

When drought years come and there are windfalls, tinder-dry duff, and masses of inflammatory material on the ground, a fire can explode into a holocaust that will burn not only debris but living trees as well, and the soil underneath them. Rains and snows may then wash the ledges clean and turn back time ten thousand years or more to the way the earth appeared after the last glacial retreat, a wilderness of sand and gravel moraine and bare exposed rock. So it has always been, over the long centuries when there was time to wait for the healing that always came.

In the Sequoias of California, where slow ground fires have periodically destroyed the small growth beneath, most of the trees bear fire scars. Before the coming of the white man they stood in open parklike groves, but when all fires were stopped, a dense understory built up for the first time in their three-thousand-year history. White and red fir, incense cedar, manzanita, and greasewood have grown into an impenetrable jungle where only sparse vegetation grew before. Should a hot, dry season come, literally charging the draws and canyons and the air above them with volatile oils and resins, the stage is set for catastrophe. A cigarette, a careless camper, or a bolt of lightning can cause an explosion, with flames leaping from the ground to the high crowns, killing the grandest trees in the world, the trees that John Muir said belong to the millennia.

In the Everglades, where man has tampered with the water supply, diverting its full cleansing flow from the prehistoric limestone drainage channels to industrial, farming, and urban developments, the glades have dried almost to the point of no return. As with the Sequoias, fire had swept over the great waving fields of sawgrass, the countless islands or hummocks, keeping invading vegetation in check. Now, when the sawgrass burns, the killing flames go down to the roots and into the scant humus over the limestone, bringing in a new mangrove ecology with the subsequent loss of myriad forms of life—the alligators, shrimp, and fish of the estuaries—and robbing food from the great flocks of ibis, flamingo, and herons once populating the region in untold millions.

I returned to the big pines and their quiet, to the slow drifting down of needles to the clean forest floor beneath them. As I looked at the great boles with their sunlit tops towering above me, I thought how good it was that they had survived, how good to see them and to know that in a few places the old ecological successions have gone on as they have for thousands of years. Their fire scars bear evidence of a power that molded man and his environment long before he learned to tame it for his needs. While man with his great machines and inventive genius for altering his living space is a major ecological force today, the elemental force of fire still molds the earth and all its life.

Fire has always molded the land and all its life, but only where the ancient cycles have not been interfered with. As a preparer of soil and healthful growth conditions for all animals and plants, fire has determined the vegetational patterns that exist in many parts of the world. It is an integral part of the ancient ecology with its checks and balances, its fragile and easily upset stability. Only when fire is recognized as an ecological force with delicately interwoven relationships binding all living things to one another and to the earth, will we begin to understand its role.

We study it today with great interest, but our perspective is still too limited, our knowledge too inadequate to give the answers. We look at it no longer as a curse but as a natural phenomenon, knowing that without it our environment would be entirely different. To exist in ecological harmony with nature, we must learn to live with fire, control it where necessary, let it run if the land and its creatures need it.

The fire scars on the old pines spoke mutely of what they had known, reminding me of what fire has meant. As I studied them I knew they posed vital questions to modern man. With his increasing occupation of the terrain, can he afford to allow areas of great recreational and resource value to burn? Can he wait for hundreds of years until the fire scars are healed and the scorched earth becomes green and verdant again? Do we question the wisdom of nature at our peril? Will we ever know enough to choose and evaluate?

The squirrel was on its way down again with the inevitable cone in its teeth. Again it stopped on the branch above me, chattering and stomping its feet. By now it accepted me as harmless, so jerked its way down the big trunk, then jumped to the ground and raced by without a glance, chose another good place to dig, and buried another treasure in the duff. The nuthatches called high above me, and the wind moaned softly through the tops as the tall trees swayed.

They had grown for two hundred years and would last another century if the fates were kind.

FOOD FOR THE FUTURE

The stand of aspen back of the beaver house looked as though a windstorm had gone through. Crisscrossed in all directions, the trees lay in total confusion. The first to fall were on the ground, others were on top of them, and some were caught against those still standing. Only the maples, birch, and a few spruces and ash remained.

I picked my way through the tangle, under and over the trunks, sometimes balancing above the ground. The cuttings were fresh, and at the base of each stump lay piles of white chips. Many of the top branches had already been gnawed off and dragged into the water along trails that were muddy and deep.

The beaver house was an old one, as high as a man and twelve to fifteen feet wide. Many generations had used it, possibly even before the aspen had come in. The top was plastered with black mud the animals had carried from the bottom of the pond, and covered with newly chewed branches which gleamed against the weathered ones of former years. When the cold came, the house would be impregnable, a frozen fortress safe from all predators except man.

In front of the house in the water were ungnawed branches, food for the future. Each addition to the pile would make those below sink more deeply beneath the level of the coming ice, but underwater entrances from the house would make all of it available. There must be enough to last the winter through, or the beaver would starve.

Once in early April, a month before the melting of the ice, I found where a beaver had left the house to find more food. Its broad, smooth trail showed it had gone inland, a desperate thing to do, for any predator could catch it with ease. That is what happened, for, on the ridge a hundred yards from the house, all that was left of the carcass were bones and bits of fur, and blood scattered on the snow.

The work went on steadily, day and night. I watched the animals at dusk, saw them swimming with branches in their mouths, heard the crashing of more trees and the slapping of their broad tails on the surface of the water when they saw me. I do not know how many beaver were there, but surely there was one old pair, together with last season's young. They would stay until the coming spring, then leave to found colonies of their own.

The red squirrels were also industrious, snipping off cones in the tops of the pines. Each time one was cut, it fell with a plop, and at times there was a steady rain of them. After a squirrel had busied itself for a while, it came to the ground to bury the harvest, putting single cones in the bed of needles and duff, underneath pieces of bark or twigs, or between rocks. Occasionally one would find a special place and pile several dozen cones in a neat mound with no covering whatsoever. I wondered, as I observed the interminable business of storage, if the animals had some secret formula for remembering things that only squirrels are heir to.

Several yellowish-white mushrooms grew on an old log. These were cut off and carried up into the trees, where they were cleverly tucked into crotches. There they would stay until wanted—a welcome change, no doubt, from the normal fare of pine seeds. I saw the squirrels hide berries the same way, and mountain ash, high-bush cranberry, Indian plums dried and withered on their stems, and even cranberries from the edge of the bog—all tucked into places where the wind and snows could not reach them.

I went to the edge of the swamp, where meadow mice lived, and explored between the dry tussocks of sedge. Down there it was dry and well protected, and in the spaces between tussocks there was a jungle of brown stems and dried blades of grass. I found the nest of a meadow mouse, a round ball of the finest bits of grass woven so intricately together that it would keep its inmate warm and still let in enough air to breathe. There were two openings, and close by was a pile of grass seeds, possibly a spoonful all told. No doubt there were many such caches located at convenient intervals along the labyrinthian network of runways through the bog. These were reserves for the future, should trailside supplies give out. Most of the winter feeding would be accomplished by foraging and hunting for seeds, but should the winter be prolonged and feeding trails encroach on another's territory, or a moose or deer walk through the swamp, destroying well-known paths, or, even worse, a weasel burrow down from the snow above to run through the maze, the little piles of seeds might prevent starvation.

Not all animals store food in the way of the beavers, squirrels, or meadow mice. Some depend entirely on feeding to repletion during the summer and fall, so they can go into hibernation or periods of slowed activity, living on stored fat in their tissues. But some predators, like the shrew, must eat their weight in flesh each day in order to provide the fuel and energy needed to keep them alive.

Each species has plans of its own peculiarly adapted to its terrain and physiological needs, but the storage instinct is deeply ingrained in all animals, especially in creatures of northern climes. None is entirely oblivious, not even man. It is natural for us to think of storing food in the fall, and there is no greater satisfaction or contentment than to know we have reserves. Even though modern man, with tin or plastic containers within easy reach, need not worry about hunger, there is comfort and even joy in laying in a supply against a long winter. And we have a concern not only for food, but for shelter and protection against bitter winds, warm clothing against subzero temperatures, and warm colors against the bleakness of snow and ice. All this is in our genes, in part of our bodies and part of our minds, an inheritance of millions of years when storage of food was a matter of life or death.

PAGES 87-98

87. A rainbow of mist from a waterfall catches the varied colors of the shore and gathers them together in its evanescent light.

88-89. A background of black stormclouds holds the threat of cold and snow above a shoreline panorama of golden birches and masses of pine.

90. Leaves of the mountain maple, in a sheltered spot away from wind and sun, glow with the extravagant colors of autumn.

91. A single bush of sumac at the end of a portage exhibits a scarlet whorl of leaves.

92-93. The brush wolf or coyote voices its haunting song at dusk or dawn in a wild, beautiful medley of music.

94-95. The ruffed grouse of upland birch and aspen groves is a symphony of color in its mottled camouflage.

96-97. Drifting aspen leaves become a golden kaleidoscope in a moving pool.

98. After the violent colors of fall, the first gentle snows come as a quiet benediction drifting softly over the leaves.

WINTER

THE FROZEN FOREST

When the snow was deep beneath the pines, I stood there, remembering how it was before the coming of the cold. A single rabbit track led off across the smooth open whiteness. The tracks were far apart, indicating great jumps sparked by fear. Clear expanses meant danger, for an owl could swoop out of the gloom on wings soft as down, an owl with clutching talons and golden eyes. I followed the tracks into a bordering swamp, a dense thicket of alder and black spruce, where the prints were close together, for the creature was feeding, had nibbled the bark of a young aspen, sampled a willow and a tip of protruding grass.

Then I saw it, a snowshoe hare, white as the snow itself, white except for its beady black eyes. At my whistle it stopped, for a whistle might herald danger, and motion attracts attention. For a moment I thought I had lost the hare, but then caught the telltale gleam of an eye and the outline of its form.

Farther on I found a place where a ruffed grouse had plunged into a snowdrift to spend the night, and in the morning had exploded out on the other side. The wing marks were plain, the tips of long primary feathers etched sharply against the snow. I broke open the drift and found the round ice-encrusted bed where it had huddled during the night. Somewhere nearby the bird was feeding on buds of aspen, balancing precariously on the high slender branches, losing its hold at times and recovering, as always, with desperate wingbeats.

The trail of a squirrel foraging for cones buried during the last frenzied days of fall led from a windfall covered with a mound of snow. Two by two, the tracks finally disappeared where the animal had burrowed down to some cache it remembered, or possibly smelled, and then had come out again to run recklessly across the open, flaunting its tail at watching enemies—perhaps a red fox, motionless and waiting to pounce, or a ghostlike ermine, or a brown marten from the treetops.

Another track started with marks of a wide spread-eagled landing, where a flying squirrel had sailed from one pine toward another and, falling short of its goal, had run frantically. During the autumn when the leaves were still yellow, I had found a drop of blood, a tiny tuft of gray fur, and the end of a tail where a great horned owl had floated out of the shadows. Now there would have been wing marks and drops of crimson against the winter whiteness.

Along the edge of the swamp, where the snowshoe hare had gone, I found the delicate tracks of a weasel, two by two again, with one foot slightly ahead of the other. They followed the border of sedges and tall grasses, then dove cleanly down into the soft snow to hunt for meadow mice in the tangle of stems. A few feet farther on, the animal came out and once more ran across the surface. I did not see the hunter, but knew what to look for: dark shiny eyes, a jet tip to the tail, a body white with the slightest tinge of ivory, like the tinge of a polar bear on the ice.

Toward the far end of the swamp I found the tracks of a moose. It had walked leisurely along, browsing on willow, striped maple, and aspen. The aspen had been straddled, the moose bending the young tree down with its enormous weight to where it could feed on the tender top branches.

The tracks of all animals moved toward the bog, where they were safer from enemies and cold and, what was more vital, found food in abundance. I kicked away the snow, then dug down to the grass and heather and found the leaves and stems were still copper in hue above the bright green of the sphagnum moss. Here was a haven for many forms of life: insects and frogs, mice, voles, and other burrowers. Close to the deep unfrozen muck, and even within it, there was protection from the cold; the light porous snow trapped the air and served as insulation for them all, ensuring survival when temperatures were far below freezing.

The cover on the forest floor is glistening and smooth, with long blue shadows reaching across it. The color now is silver and blue. It looks as though nothing were happening, and, were it not for the tracks of non-hibernating creatures, one might think it sterile and devoid of life, sealed by the elements in a deep unchangeable freeze.

One night when it was twenty degrees below zero, I stood among the trees and listened. There were several sharp reports, the expansion of ice and the cracking of fibers in tree trunks heavy with moisture and bound by hard, impervious coverings of bark. Sometimes the sounds are like pistol shots, but there are also small cracklings and rustlings so nearly inaudible that at times one can barely hear them. There are always sounds in a frozen forest, for freezing means expansion, and when tissues expand, they break. Frost has the same action on rocks, forcing them apart, breaking particles and making new soil, but the grand sounds are the rumbling thunder of the lakes when the forming ice grows thick, when it secures the islands, the rocks, and the points.

A flock of black-capped chickadees flew in, calling and chattering as only chickadees can, generating so much warmth they seemed oblivious to the cold. They explored the bark of trees for eggs and hidden insects, fluttered and scurried about in frenzied busyness, and all the time sounded their merry *chickadee-dee-dee,* and even hints of their long mating call as the sun burst from the clouds.

High up in a spruce, pine siskins were examining the cones for seeds, and from the brown top came a cascade of tiny bracts and scales. They too were busy, and from them came a faint, almost demure *tseeping* that belied their furious energy.

As I watched them, I wondered how it would be at night when they were still. They would no doubt crowd together in some dense cover for mutual warmth, with feathers fluffed out to trap and hold the warmth of their tiny bodies. Sometimes the snow would cover them, as I had let it cover me at times, for snow is aerated and warm. Husky dogs know the secret and sleep warmly all night long with fur fluffed, noses tucked in, and the blanket of snow over and around them. Only when an animal is exposed does it suffer. Dogs survive, as do all other furred and downy creatures: the rabbits, partridge, songbirds, and the woodpeckers in their holes. Eskimos, with loose fur clothing tied tightly around necks, wrists, and ankles, keep warm in the same way. Survival is no problem if body warmth can be trapped and held.

But many creatures, instead of fighting the bitter cold, go to sleep. Some animals, like the skunk and chipmunk, remain dormant during most of the winter but may come out during warm spells or thaws, returning to their dens with a change in temperature, to sleep once more. True hibernators—jumping mice, woodchucks, and bears—spend the winter in dry, protected places, often underground in burrows or caves, or in shelters beneath windfalls, logs, or shelving ledges of rock. Bats hibernate too, but most migrate at the approach of winter. Frogs, reptiles, salamanders, earthworms, and insects seldom come into the open even on the warmest days. They go into the long sleep as all hibernators do, with body temperatures low, heartbeats slowed, oxygen requirements at a minimum, conserving warmth and energy and depending on the stored fat in their tissues to carry them through.

There is a withdrawal and a resting in the frozen forest, but also a changing and conditioning in preparation for the spring to come. The forest depends on winter for fulfillment, just as it does on the seasons of growth. Who knows what goes on during the long sleep—the recharging of energies used so lavishly during the spring, summer, and fall, the slow maturing of organs and tissues, of sperms and eggs, of spores and seeds, and of young conceived before hibernation?

We do know that low temperatures and darkness are often necessary for the growth of spores, seeds, and bulbs, that without the freezing process some species may not survive to grow in the spring. Even cocoons gathered in the fall must have a period of cold if the moths are to emerge perfect.

Changing temperatures, lowering humidity, loss of sunlight during the last weeks of fall, all stimulate color changes, the growth of long guard hairs and of warm insulating down close to the skin of mammals and birds. In reverse, and as winter wanes, colors return, guard hairs disappear, and down grows thinner. Some cancer cells are activated into growth when chilled, and florists know that certain flowers need a period of cold and dark if they are to bloom with the advent of warmth and more daylight.

The shortening of the dark days causes glandular changes in all creatures, stimulating some to migrate, others to go into hibernation. Again in reverse, when birds who have spent the winter in the south begin to feel the impact of lengthening days and growing light intensity, such cyclic phenomena signal that the time has come to move back north once again.

In the frozen forest, as spring approaches, even though animals may be asleep, the signals grow clearer and clearer until their awakening and almost drugged emergence into the world of sunlight and warmth. The timeclock of the seasons is infallible, and all creatures of the earth respond, under the palms and tropical jungles of the south or in a northern forest world of silver and blue. Wherever they are, the changes come, changes and reactions that have been in the building for millions of years, all part of an over-all design woven into the genetic matrix of living things.

CAMOUFLAGE

As the weather grew colder, there was a gradual change in the coloration of rabbits and weasels, an uneven splotching of brown and white that matched the scattered patches of newly fallen snow. When winter finally came, with its smooth unbroken drifts, both animals were completely white, with the exception of the weasel's tail, which was tipped with jet black, and of a fine pinstripe of black along the inside tips of the rabbit's ears. But why that single touch of jet, or the black-tipped wings of the snow goose, or the white tip of a fox's tail? I could not even guess, unless it was a distraction from the impact of solid color.

I thought, as I watched a rabbit scampering over deep snow on its splayed snowshoe feet, of the great snowy owls of the Arctic drifting down to the northern states when lemmings are scarce on the bleak frozen tundras, of white arctic foxes, of polar bears on blue-white ice floes or on the coasts where they bear their young, and of ptarmigan changing their brief summer color of speckled brown and white to almost total white during the winter.

I remembered a host of other creatures seen during the summer: a fawn which was dappled like the sunlight falling on brown leaves; partridge chicks that had hidden swiftly under dead leaves until they seemed to disappear before my eyes; a leopard frog whose mottled green and brown confused such enemies as blue herons standing in the shallows, and whose creamy underside protected it from marauding fish looking up at the white glare of sunlight; a tiny tree frog which remained all but invisible on the branch of a cedar until it moved; a spotted pike concealed by the sunlit tangles of water plants—each species part of the environmental color scheme.

All this was difficult to explain, for man sees colors, combinations, and designs differently from other creatures. What may look bright red, orange, or black to us may not be what other animals see. The ability to change colors almost instantly or over a period of time is a physiological response to light and dark, to seasonal changes and to metabolic requirements, not only in animals but plants as well.

What actually takes place through the physics of light, body chemistry, hormonic change, and response is still beyond us. We know that over the eons of evolutional progression those species survived who were best adapted to the color patterns around them. Originally there may have been an almost unnoticeable variation, possibly a slight mutation or an accidental or fortuitous combination of genes, but whatever the explanation, it gave certain individuals a slight advantage over their kind in escaping enemies, enough perhaps to make survival possible, with adaptations inevitably becoming part of the genetic pool of the race.

Protective color changes are as wonderful in animals as they are in flowers and leaves, just as involved and complex as the mating habits of many species and the changing coloration that occurs as breeding times approach. Such phenomena are some of the secrets of the hidden forest, secrets most of us take for granted. Evolving over untold millions of years and keeping pace with changing environmental conditions, camouflage, mimicry, and sexual adornment are miracles of adjustment and adaptation.

WINTER HAZARDS

During the warm months of the year, availability of food is seldom a deciding factor in survival, unless terrain has been disturbed by man. It is during the winter that the great decisions of life or death are made, for with the coming of the deep snows and the periods of extreme cold, the free movements of animals are limited, and much of their normal food supplies is hidden from view or becomes unobtainable.

This is particularly true of deer, for when snows are deep they are forced to yard up in extremely limited areas, sometimes in swamps or sheltered pockets of lowland, where they feed on the browse that is within reach. As time goes on, their trails become deeper and deeper, and branches are sometimes picked clean long before the coming of spring. Because it is very difficult for deer to travel through snow that is belly deep or even deeper, they seldom leave the protection of yards, in spite of growing scarcity of food and impending starvation, for fear of being caught by their enemies, enemies who can travel freely as spring approaches and crusts form on the snow.

Where deer have eaten the lower branches of cedar along the lakeshores, the browse line looks from a distance as though the trees had been trimmed with a clipper. While some lakeshore feeding goes on during the winter, it is usually done while animals can still move without hindrance. Heavily browsed yards look the same, no matter where they may be.

Yards have other hazards as well, for sometimes wolves, coyotes, or lynxes jump down onto the hardbeaten trails of a yard in an attempt to drive the deer into the snow, where they will be helpless. But tables are turned occasionally, when a frantic buck or a doe with a yearling fawn slashes an attacker with its sharp, knifelike front hooves.

Many people think there is always plenty of food in any woods, but browsing animals must find special types suited to their needs: mountain maple, cedar, balsam, the tips of young birches and aspen, dogwood, and alder. When such foods grow scarce, or beyond the reach of deer even when they are standing on their hind legs, the animals will starve, no matter how luxuriant other growths may be.

Partridge have no problem, for they are bud-feeders and glean in the tops of trees. Beaver, if they have failed to store enough aspen, birch, or alder branches in the deep water around their houses, are sometimes forced to leave protection and make forays that might lead to tragedy.

Porcupines, being bark-eaters, can spend the entire winter in a clump of pine or spruce, gnawing great patches off the upper trunks, causing mutilation or even death of the trees. In Alaska there is an area called the Porcupine Forest, where all the spruces are dead, the silvery weatherbeaten trunks evidence of what porcupines can do when their enemies are no longer able to keep the population in check.

Squirrels who have stored vast quantities of cones sometimes find the snow too deep or heavily crusted for them to burrow down to their caches. However, within migration range there are usually stands of jack pine where the hard unopened cones and the seeds they bear are fastened securely to the branches.

Fish often suffer when they are caught with ice forming clear to the bottom of shallow ponds. Just as dangerous to them is the loss of oxygen which results from a lack of circulation of the water or heavy concentrations of fish in small areas. Winter kills are inevitable in situations such as this, and, when trapped by early freezing, fish are often doomed.

Winter means challenge and hazard. While most creatures of the forest make adequate preparation, there are often conditions beyond their control that determine whether they live or die, precipitating the inexorable weeding-out of those who are not as strong or resistant as others. Predators are subject to the same controls as those they prey upon, in a balanced and sound relationship that has as its ultimate objective a thriving ecological plateau.

PAGES 109-120

109. Although the larger snowshoe hare is a lesson in adaptive coloration, the cottontail changes little at the approach of winter.

110-111. With grasses brown and sere, dogwoods red, and birches forming bare traceries against the background of fallen leaves, the forest waits for the snow.

112-113. A buck with a fine spread of antlers comes to the creek to drink. In a few weeks, as the snow builds up, he will yard for the winter in some deep, protected lowland.

114-115. In freezing pools, the patterns of crystals shift constantly. At dusk, when it is quiet, the growing spears of ice move and touch one another with a gentle tinkling like the music of tiny bells.

116-117. The natural beauty of dogwood stems against the snow evokes the studied simplicity of a Japanese print.

118-119. When winter really comes, the forest lies withdrawn, resting beneath a blanket of snow.

120. A ruffed grouse, exploding from its warm nest in a snowdrift, has marked the opening with the tips of its wings.

EPILOGUE

WILDERNESS, A HUMAN NEED

For millions of years man shared ancient ecological balances and relationships with other creatures in a common environment. He is therefore physiologically and spiritually part of a primeval past, still attuned to nature and never quite happy or content removed from its influences. Man became human because of the development of his brain, his ability to adapt himself to new situations, and the slow growth of awareness and perception. In spite of his sophistication and inventive genius, he still does not understand or appreciate the importance of natural beauty and of preserving some areas where the ancient scene is undisturbed.

Deep down in his subconscious, a part of his pool of racial memories is an abiding sense of oneness with life he cannot deny. Within him is a hunger and a craving for wildness and nature, which he cannot quite understand. He must feel the ground under his feet, use muscles as they were meant to be used, know the warmth and light of wood fires in primitive shelters away from storms. He must feel old rhythms, the cyclic change of seasons, see the miracles of growth, and sense the issues of life and death. He is, in spite of himself, still a creature of forests and open meadows, of rivers, lakes, and seashores. He needs to look at sunsets and sunrises and the coming of a full moon. Although he is conquering space and producing life, ancient needs and longings are still part of him, and in his urbanized technological civilization he still listens to the song of the wilderness.

The hidden forest in all its vagaries, its many facets, and its amazing interdependencies, is part of him. The forest is more than trees, soil, and water, far more than can ever be seen. It is a place where he can sense the world as it used to be, a sanctuary of the spirit where he can find himself in an eroding environment where the old values are being lost—the values that made him what he is.

In our swiftly growing civilization, with its new cities and communities and pyramiding industrial uses polluting the air, soil, and water and bringing ugliness to places of beauty, man's problems are very real. The vast concentrations of people in inhuman megalopolises, removed from a natural to an increasingly artificial environment, make the preservation of wild or unblemished areas of inestimable value.

Such places should be reserved from development or exploitation for the simple reason that they are needed by modern man for solace and balance. No trees should be cut there, no machines allowed to scar the earth's surface, no pollution permitted, no wild creatures or vegetation eliminated. Disturb such places in the slightest, and they lose their value. In the face of the imbalance, man's spirit shrivels, for only in nature can he gain perspective.

It has been said that beauty is in the eye of the beholder and that it is its own excuse for being. Man needs beauty as he needs food. He is constantly in search of it. Artists spend their lives creating it, but for the vast majority it lies in the simplicities of natural things. Ugliness is revolting to man, but beauty sustains him. The hidden forest is vital to man's happiness, but only by being aware of the unseen forces at work within it can he truly appreciate its worth.

ABOUT THE PHOTOGRAPHY

ABOUT THE PHOTOGRAPHY

BY LES BLACKLOCK

Most people I meet, upon learning that I am a wildlife photographer, are apt to remark that the job must take infinite patience and that they just don't have that kind of patience. And I'm apt to answer that hunting with a camera is as exciting as hunting with a gun, and gun hunters stalk game for hours, even days, with no feeling of being especially patient.

But if someone were to say that photography of vegetation takes patience (no one ever does), I couldn't agree more. It seemed, when I was shooting the hundreds of transparencies aimed at *The Hidden Forest,* that most subjects that appealed to me were at the end of a long wispy stem or branch, and that every day was windy.

Why didn't I cut the branch and bring it into a studio, where I would have no wind, a choice of colored backgrounds, and complete control of light? Because that approach would have cost the feeling of "being there," of seeing things as they are—of believability.

So I went to the other extreme. Before I started photography for this book, I made a rule for myself that I would not move nature around to "create" a composition; I must shoot my subjects as I found them. Only with such a purist attitude could I portray nature as it is. If foliage in these pictures is wet, it is wet from rain or dew, not from a spray gun.

So sometimes I found myself kneeling or lying in water for hours, waiting for the right combination of forest-filtered sunlight and *no wind,* in order to photograph fragile flowers or moss. Other times I stood uncomfortably in a half-crouch while red maple leaves refused to hold still for a one-second exposure. Often I pressed the plunger on my cable release when movement stopped, only to see—or think I saw—movement during the exposure. So I exposed many sheets of film, hoping that the flower or leaf remained still long enough to create a sharp image on one of them.

Most of the photography in this book, and all of the close-up photography of vegetation, was done with a Calumet view camera on 4x5 Ektachrome daylight film, through a Schneider-Kreusnach Symmar 6″ lens. I employed the swings and tilts of the camera to control my plane of focus on every exposure. The camera was mounted on a Professional Jr. tripod, a heavy wooden-legged motion-picture tripod which gave me the solid foundation I needed for exposures that sometimes lasted eight seconds. My exposure meter was a Sekonic incident-light meter. This is an old friend, since it was first introduced as the "Norwood" many years ago. And I treat it as an old friend, believing everything it says, but interpreting its suggested exposure to fit my experience in varying situations.

I cheat a little when using the view camera or Speed Graphic; I use a 5-by-7-inch mirror to reflect the picture from the ground glass, so I can see my composition right-side-up.

Most of the wildlife photographs were made with an old and battered series D 4x5 Graflex. How I wish that great camera were still being manufactured! A 36cm Schneider Xenar lens enlarges the image to twice normal size, which means I must be closer than fifty feet for most big-game pictures, and about five feet for small wildlife.

The red squirrel and Cape May warbler were photographed with a 35mm Nikkormat camera and 300mm Nikkor-P Auto lens, on Ektachrome X film. An old Leica with a 135mm Hector lens felled the ruffed grouse on Kodachrome.

The spotted fawn wouldn't hold still long enough to maneuver a tripod-mounted camera, so I hand-held a Kodak Medalist (2¼x3¼) for that picture.

As a wildlife photographer I have, through the years, become increasingly appreciative of the intimate detail and intricate designs which I found in my forest "studio." I noticed that casual visitors to the north woods were amazed when I pointed out the fragile beauty beneath their feet and all around them as they walked through the forest. I have long wished that I could share what I see and love in the forest with more people. So I am grateful for the opportunity to bring some glimpses of the forest world—either new or familiar—to readers of this book. It has been my good fortune to have Sigurd Olson as my partner in this exploration of the forest.

As our joint effort started, Sigurd Olson keyed his essays to my first pictures, and I found myself trying in turn to get pictures that would illustrate his writing. We soon found that this approach hampered our creativity, so began to work independently. We were in constant communication, however; each knew what the other was doing, and we could wander everywhere without restrictions. Some of the fondest recollections I have are of the period we worked together on this book, and I am eternally grateful for the privilege of collaborating with a man whose first-hand knowledge and understanding of the woods and their ways are probably second to none.